# The Terrible EEK

# The Terrible EEK

A Japanese Tale Retold by Patricia A. Compton ▪ illustrated by Sheila Hamanaka

SIMON & SCHUSTER BOOKS FOR YOUNG READERS

Published by Simon & Schuster

New York · London · Toronto · Sydney · Tokyo · Singapore

SIMON & SCHUSTER BOOKS FOR YOUNG READERS
Simon & Schuster Building, Rockefeller Center
1230 Avenue of the Americas, New York, New York 10020
Text copyright © 1991 by Patricia A. Compton. Illustrations copyright © 1991 by Sheila Hamanaka.
All rights reserved including the right of reproduction in whole or in part in any form.
SIMON & SCHUSTER BOOKS FOR YOUNG READERS is a trademark of Simon & Schuster.

Designed by Lucille Chomowicz.
The text of this book is set in Trump.
The illustrations were done in oil paint.
Manufactured in the United States of America. 10 9 8 7 6 5 4 3 2 1

Library of Congress Cataloging-in-Publication Data: Compton, Patricia A. The terrible eek / retold by
Patricia A. Compton: illustrated by Sheila Hamanaka. Retold from a Japanese folktale. Summary: A father's
fear of the terrible leak ultimately saves him from a thief and wolf. [1. Folklore—Japan.] I. Hamanaka,
Sheila, ill. II. Title. PZ8.1.C738Ts 1991 398.2—dc20 [E] 91-8421 AC
ISBN 0-671-73737-6

For my husband, Jim, my traveling companion — PC

For Suzy and Kiyo — SH

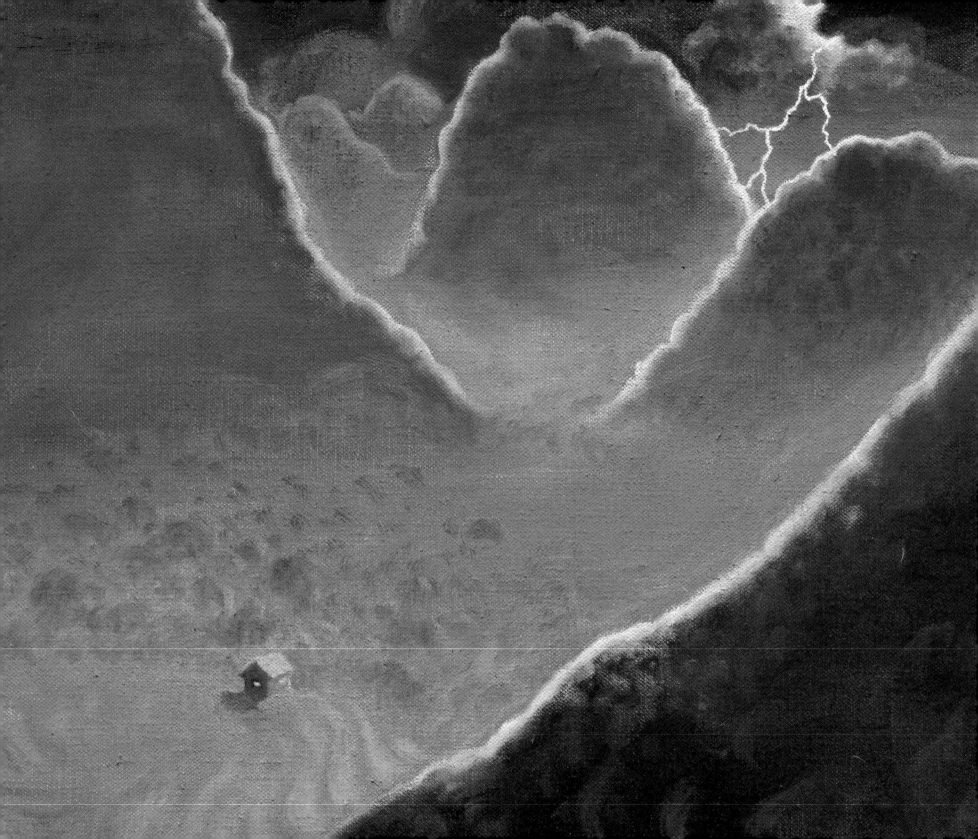

A long time ago, in a certain place in the mountains, it began to rain. The wind shook a small house with a thatch roof.

Inside, a boy and his father sat warming their hands over a small fire. Nearby, the boy's mother prepared the evening meal.

The sounds of the wind and rain battering at the house frightened the little boy. "Father, are you ever afraid?" the boy asked.

"Yes, my son, there are things that I fear," the father answered.

"What do you fear most?" the boy asked.

"Among humans," the father replied, "I am most afraid of a thief."

It happened that a thief had climbed on to the thatch roof of the house and was hiding up there. When the thief heard the father's reply, he was triumphant. "I am the strongest and most fearsome of creatures," he said to himself. "I am what they are most afraid of."

"Among animals," the father continued, "I am most afraid of the wolf."

At that very moment, a wolf was sneaking by the side of the house with plans to steal a chicken or two for his dinner.

The wolf sniffed haughtily and said to himself, "I am the strongest and most fearsome of creatures. I am what they are most afraid of."

"But the most frightening thing of all to me," the father went on telling his son, "is a terrible leak. I hope there are no leaks tonight."

The wolf stopped a moment and thought, "What is a terrible leak?" He had never heard of a terrible leak. It must be an awful creature if they are most afraid of it.

A noisy gust of wind blew away some of the sounds of the father's words before they reached the thief on the roof. All he heard was "…the most frightening thing of all is a terrible eek."

The thief wondered what a terrible eek could be. He reached up to scratch his head and lost his balance. Then he slipped on the wet thatch and slid off the roof, landing right on the back of the wolf.

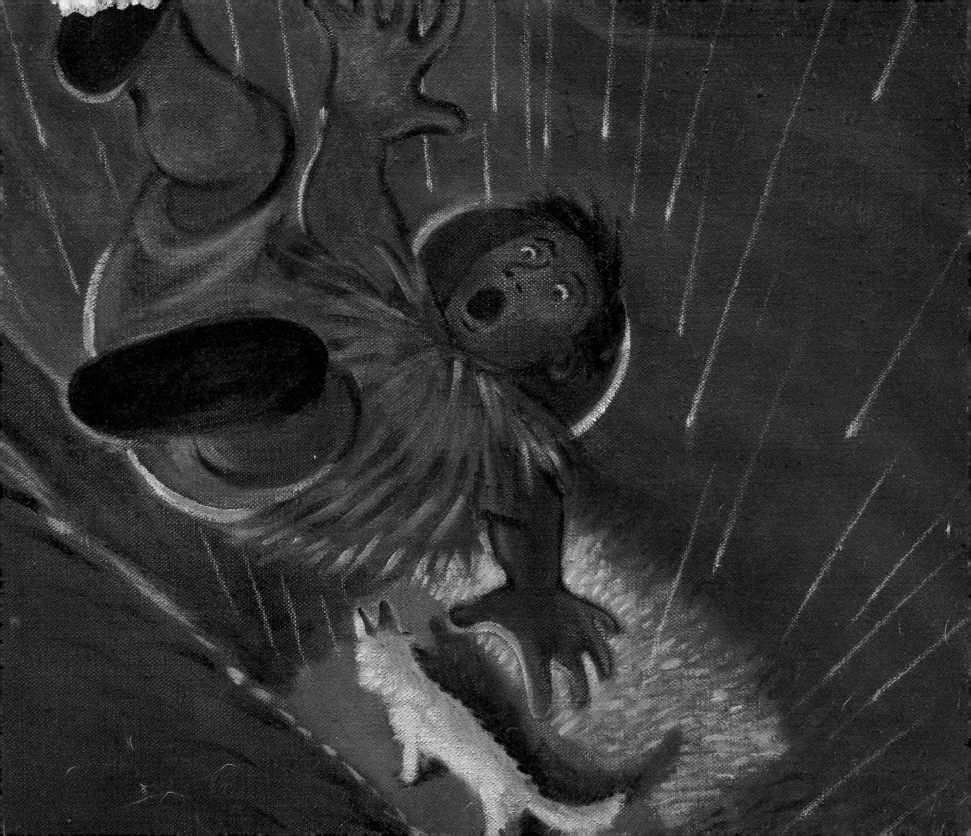

Now the poor thief
thought he had landed
on the back of the terrible
eek. And the wolf thought
that the terrible leak had
landed on him.

The wolf howled, then
ran with all his might
toward the woods. He
was hoping the terrible
leak would fall off. The
thief clutched the wolf's
neck and hung on with
all his might.

As they sped through the forest, the thief saw a low-hanging branch.

In one quick motion, he let go of the wolf's neck, grabbed the branch, and swung free.

The thief was so relieved to be away from the terrible eek that he did not notice that the branch was too weak to hold him. It cracked and he fell.

It happened that there was a deep hole right under the tree. The thief tumbled into the hole and could not climb up the steep, slippery sides.

The wolf, feeling the weight leave his back, ran to his den. Once there he collapsed, completely out of breath. After the wolf finally caught his breath, he felt very thirsty. He peered cautiously out of his den. Not seeing anything, he went to the water hole for a drink. There he met a tiger.

"Tiger, do you know what a terrible leak is?" asked the wolf. "Humans fear it more than anything. It jumped on my back and nearly choked me to death. Will you help me catch the leak?"

"I have never heard of a terrible leak. I thought I was the strongest and most frightening creature in the world," the tiger said. "Yes, I will go with you to catch the terrible leak."

A monkey sitting in a nearby tree heard the tiger and the wolf talking. "Where are you going?" he asked.

"We are going to catch the terrible leak," said the tiger. "Will you come along and help us?"

"I have never heard of a terrible leak, and I am not strong and frightening like you are," said the monkey, "but I am clever. So I will come and help you catch it."

The tiger and the monkey followed the wolf back to the tree where the terrible leak had jumped off the wolf's back.

The monkey found the big hole under the tree and said, "I will put my tail down into the hole and see if the leak tries to grab it."

"Are you there, terrible leak?" cried the monkey, lowering his tail into the hole.

When the thief saw the
monkey's tail, he grabbed
tight and pulled.

The monkey became
very frightened, and he
pulled with all his might.
The monkey pulled the
thief right out of the hole.

The tiger roared,

the wolf howled,

the monkey screeched,

and the thief yelled.

This awful noise frightened them all so much that they ran off into the woods and never ever found out about the terrible leak.

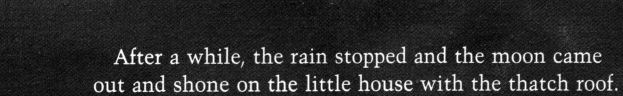

After a while, the rain stopped and the moon came
out and shone on the little house with the thatch roof.

The boy and his mother and father were
sound asleep in their dry, warm beds.